DARK HUNTER
CROW HALL

First published 2015 by
A & C Black, an imprint of Bloomsbury Publishing Plc
50 Bedford Square, London, WC1B 3DP

www.bloomsbury.com

Bloomsbury is a registered trademark of Bloomsbury Publishing Plc

A CIP catalogue for this book is available from the British Library

ISBN: 978–1-4729–0816–2

Printed and bound in Great Britain by CPI Group (UK) Ltd,
Croydon CR0 4YY

13 5 7 9 10 8 6 4 2

DARK HUNTER

CROW HALL

BENJAMIN HULME-CROSS

ILLUSTRATED BY NELSON EVERGREEN

A & C BLACK
AN IMPRINT OF BLOOMSBURY
LONDON NEW DELHI NEW YORK SYDNEY

The Dark Hunter

Mr Daniel Blood is the Dark Hunter.
People call him to fight evil demons,
vampires and ghosts.

Edgar and Mary help Mr Blood
with his work.

The three hunters need to be strong and
clever to survive...

Contents

Chapter 1   The Letter   7

Chapter 2   Dust and Darkness   17

Chapter 3   The Search   25

Chapter 4   The Painting   34

Chapter 5   The Crow   43

Chapter 1

The Letter

Mr Blood, Edgar and Mary stood outside the gates to Crow Hall. Mr Blood shouted again and again. Nobody came to let them in.

Up in the sky, a pale moon shone down on the hall's black towers.

"Are you sure this is the right place?" Edgar asked.

"This is the right place," Mr Blood replied. He pointed up at two large stone crows that stood on top of the gateposts. "The letter told us to come to Crow Hall."

"Who sent the letter?" asked Edgar.

"At the bottom of the letter are the initials, 'C. H.'" Mr Blood said.

"The letter said the house was haunted," said Mary. "Maybe C. H. is in trouble inside the house."

"We will have to climb over the gates and bang on the door," said Mr Blood.

Mr Blood began climbing up the black iron gates. Mary went after him. Edgar looked up at the sharp metal spikes on top of the gates. "Are you sure this is a good idea?" he asked.

"Come on!" Mr Blood called from the other side of the gates.

They walked up the path to the main door. There were two more crows carved into the black wood of the door.

Mr Blood banged on the door with his stick. There was no answer.

"There is no-one here," said Edgar. "Let's go home."

Mr Blood ignored him and knocked again.

Mary turned to Edgar. "Don't you want to know what's going on?" she asked.

"I'm not bothered," said Edgar as he turned around to stare back at the gates. He couldn't see the stone crows on top of the gate posts.

"That's odd," he thought.

"Right," said Mr Blood. "We will have to force our way in. C. H. could be in danger and we must act."

He turned the heavy iron door handle. Edgar held his breath. To everyone's surprise the door swung open with a loud creak. It sounded like the screech of a crow.

Chapter 2

Dust and Darkness

It was pitch black inside the hall.

Mr Blood lifted three candles out of his bag. He lit them and gave one each to Edgar and Mary. Everything was covered in dust. Nobody had been there for a very long time.

Edgar looked out of one of the windows. He saw a pair of crows in a tree. It looked like they were watching him. He looked away and then looked back again. The crows had gone.

"If the house is haunted we must find the place where the ghost is strongest," said Mr Blood. "What have I told you about where a ghost has the most power?"

"The place where the person died," said Edgar with a shiver.

Mr Blood smiled at Edgar and nodded.

Suddenly, there was a loud bang. Edgar and Mary jumped with fright. The front door had slammed shut. All three candles went out.

"It was just the wind," said Mary. She didn't sound very sure.

Then they heard a strange sound in the dark.

"What's that?" asked Edgar. At first the sound was a gentle flutter. Then the noise grew louder.

"It sounds like the beating of wings," whispered Mary.

The sound grew louder and louder. It was as if the room was full of huge birds. Mary felt feathers brushing against her face. She screamed. A terrible screech filled the air.

Then the room was silent again.

Mr Blood lit his candle and found Mary. She lit her candle and they looked around the room. The dust had not been disturbed. There were no birds in the room.

But something was missing. Mary gave a cry. Edgar had gone!

Chapter 3

The Search

"Edgar? Edgar!" Mary called. There was no reply.

Mr Blood pulled out a length of rope from his bag. He tied one end of the rope around his waist, and the other end around Mary's waist.

"We must stay with each other," he said.

"Where can he be?" Mary asked. "Can ghosts make people vanish?"

"I don't know," said Mr Blood. "This is a very odd ghost. We must carry on. We must find the place where the ghost is strongest. That is where Edgar will be."

Mary and Mr Blood walked along the ground floor going into each room. They looked in cupboards. They opened chests. They broke down the door to the cellar. There was no sign of Edgar.

Mary and Mr Blood walked back to the hall where Edgar had vanished. Mr Blood turned to go up the main stairs.

"Wait," Mary said. She pointed at two large stone crows on short posts on either side of the stairs.

"Were they there before?" Mary asked.

Mr Blood frowned. "I can't be sure," he said. "It was so dark. I didn't notice them. But come. We must carry on and search the rest of the house."

They began to climb the stairs. They had only taken three steps when Mary tripped on the rope and slipped back to the bottom.

"Are you hurt?" asked Mr Blood. Mary shook her head and got to her feet.

She looked at the stone crows and let out a scream. The two statues had turned around. They were no longer facing the door. They were staring at Mary. She felt sick with fear.

"Come on!" shouted Mr Blood. "We must find Edgar." Again they began to climb the stairs. As they did so, they heard the screech of crows.

Chapter 4

The Painting

As they reached the landing of the first floor, the sound of screeching stopped. In front of them was a painting of the head of a crow.

Its beak was closed and its head was looking down. It looked as if it were about to stab down at something with its beak. Its huge, black eye stared at Mary.

"Look," said Mr Blood. He pointed at the bottom corner of the painting. The artist had marked the picture with his initials – C. H.

"Maybe C. H. is the ghost," Mary said in a low voice.

"I don't think that we are dealing with a ghost," said Mr Blood. "I believe that something else has control of this place. Something... bigger."

"Let's just find Edgar and get out of here," Mary said.

They went from room to room. They
looked for secret doors behind shelves.
They lifted carpets to look for trapdoors.
They called out Edgar's name over and
over again. And every time they called,
they heard the screech of crows in reply.

They walked past two suits of armour, both holding spears. Mr Blood and Mary took a spear each and Mary felt a little safer.

But, as they returned to the landing, Mary's eyes went wide with terror.

Again she screamed, and again they heard the screech of crows. Mr Blood looked up at the painting and his jaw dropped. The picture had changed.

Now, the painting was not just of
the crow's head, it was of the whole of the
crow. Its wings were spread out wide. Its
beak was open. It stood over the body
of a boy. And the boy in the painting
was Edgar!

Chapter 5

The Crow

Mary burst into tears. Mr Blood put his arm around her.

"I believe Edgar is still alive," said Mr Blood. "But we must try to make sense of what we have seen."

"It's something to do with crows," said Mary.

"And art," said Mr Blood. "The statues. The painting. This is no ghost. It may be the house itself that is doing this."

"The letter and the painting were both signed C.H." Mary said.

"I've been a fool!" Mr Blood said. "C. H. must stand for Crow Hall! It is the house itself that is the evil here."

Mr Blood grabbed Mary by the hand and they hurried to the stairs.

"We need to get to the top," he said. "A creature with wings – it would live at the top!"

They ran up as fast as they could up the stairs, gripping their spears.

They raced from one room to the next until they came to the end of the corridor. In front of them was a huge mirror. Mr Blood ran his hand around the mirror frame. Mary looked in the mirror and saw something coming, behind them.

"Look out!" cried Mary. The two stone crows were flying through the air towards them. Mr Blood raised his spear and Mary threw herself to the floor. As she fell, the rope that tied her to Mr Blood pulled him over too.

The crows screeched overhead and smashed into the mirror. Glass and stone pieces tumbled to the floor and then the corridor was silent again.

In place of the broken mirror, they now saw a set of narrow stairs.

Mr Blood led the way up to a door
at the top of the stairs. He opened it and
they both stepped through into a large,
cold room.

Edgar lay on a slab of stone in the
middle of the room. He wasn't moving.

A huge crow sat on his chest. Blood dripped from its beak. There were wounds to Edgar's neck. The screech of the crow grew louder and louder.

Mr Blood and Mary dropped their spears and fell to their knees, covering their ears to block out the evil sound. The crow opened its beak wider and wider. Mary felt that the screeching sound was drilling right into her brain.

She reached down for her spear. The
crow's great, black eyes seemed to grow
wider. Mary hurled the spear.

It flew at the crow's open beak and
went down its throat. The screech
stopped at once.

The candles blew out and the sound of wings came back. Mary felt feathers on her face. She screamed until the sound of wings stopped.

Mr Blood lit his candle and Mary held her breath.

The floor was covered in black feathers and black blood. The crow was dead. And Edgar was slowly sitting up.

"Why did the house send you the letter?" asked Mary as they walked away from Crow Hall.

"I fear it had evil plans. It wanted more victims," said Mr Blood.

"And it nearly had one," said Edgar rubbing his neck.

"But how can a house become evil?" asked Mary.

"Sometimes, when terrible evil has taken place in a house, the house itself becomes a force for evil," said Mr Blood.

"So the crows were just the form the evil took?" asked Mary.

"You are wise," said Mr Blood smiling at her. "And you are brave," he said to Edgar. Edgar gave a broad grin.

Six thrilling new adventures for the DARK HUNTER!

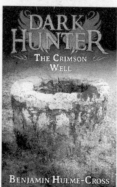